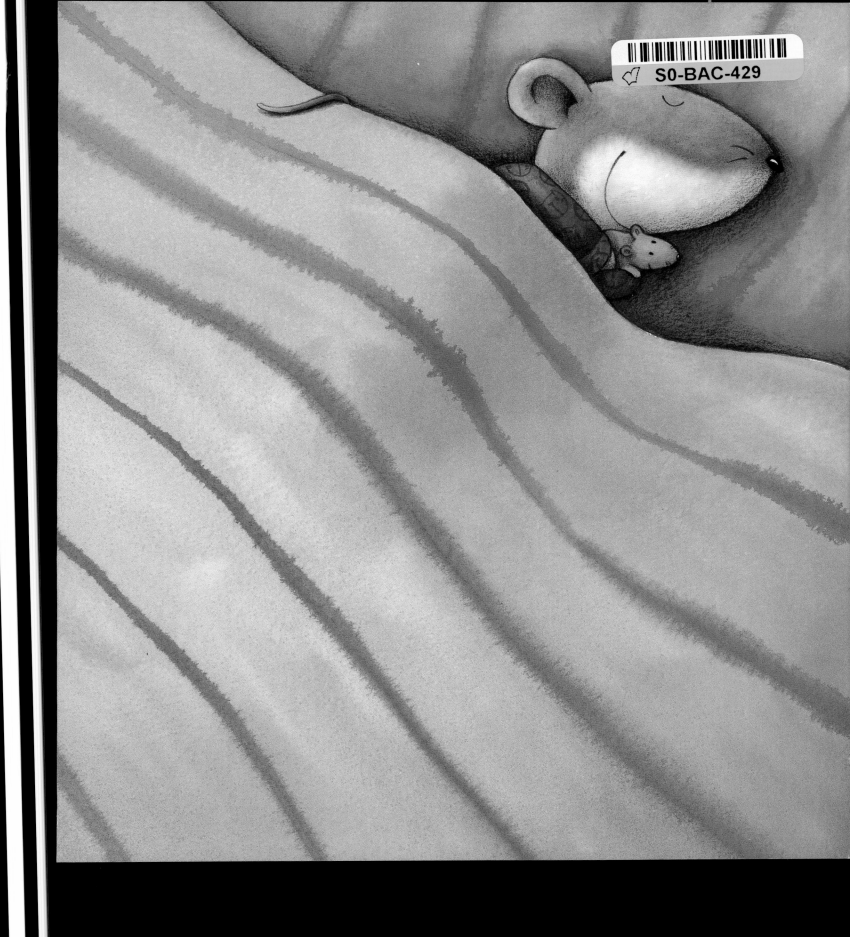

For my Parents S.R.

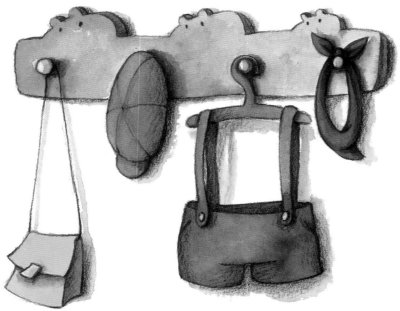

a minedition book
published by Penguin Young Readers Group

Text copyright © 2004 by Brigitte Weninger
Illustrations copyright © 2004 by Stephanie Roehe
First American edition, 2005
First published in German under the original title: MIKO „Mama Aufstehen, Spielen!"
translated by Charise Myngheer
Coproduction with Michael Neugebauer Publishing Ltd. Hong Kong.
ISBN 0-698-40012-7

Manufactured in Hong Kong by Wide World Ltd.
Designed by Michael Neugebauer
Typesetting in Kidprint MT
Color separation by Fotoreproduzioni Grafiche, Verona, Italy.
Library of Congress Cataloging-in-Publication Data available upon request.

10 9 8 7 6 5 4 3 2 1
First Impression

Brigitte Weninger

MiKO

"Mom,
Wake Up
and Play!"

Illustrated by
Stephanie Roehe

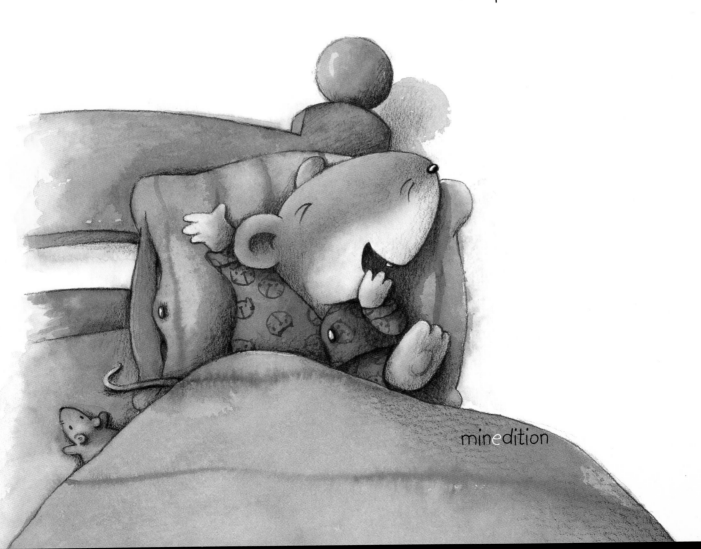

minedition

Miko woke up early.
"Mimiki, now we have lots of time to play!
Let's go wake Mom."

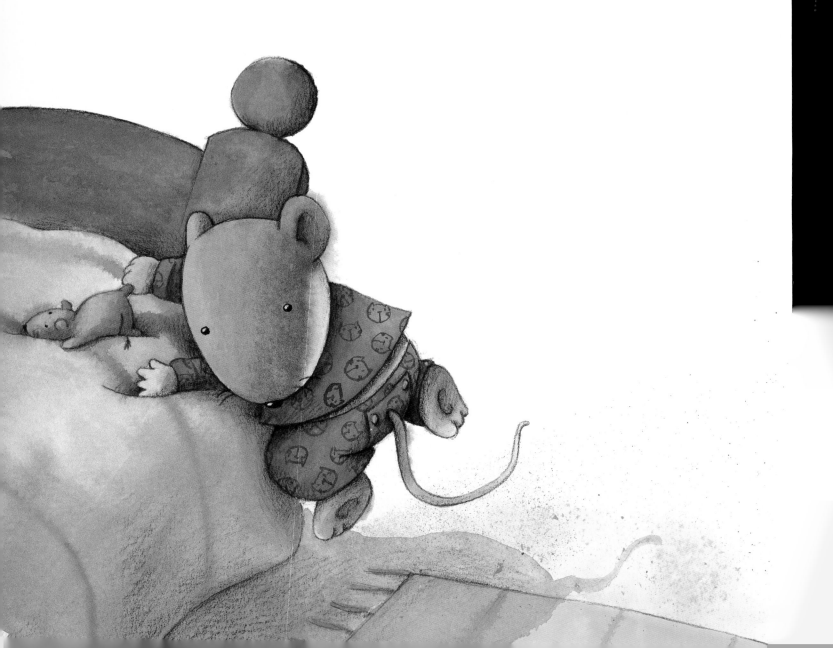

"Wake up, Mom!" Miko said.

Mom didn't move.

"Mom, wake up! Let's play," said Miko again.

"Don't you want to play with me?"

"Nuhhhh...," mumbled Mom out from under the blanket.

"Not yet. Can I sleep until the alarm clock rings?

Pleasssse?" begged Mom.

"Okay," answered Miko. "We'll let you sleep."

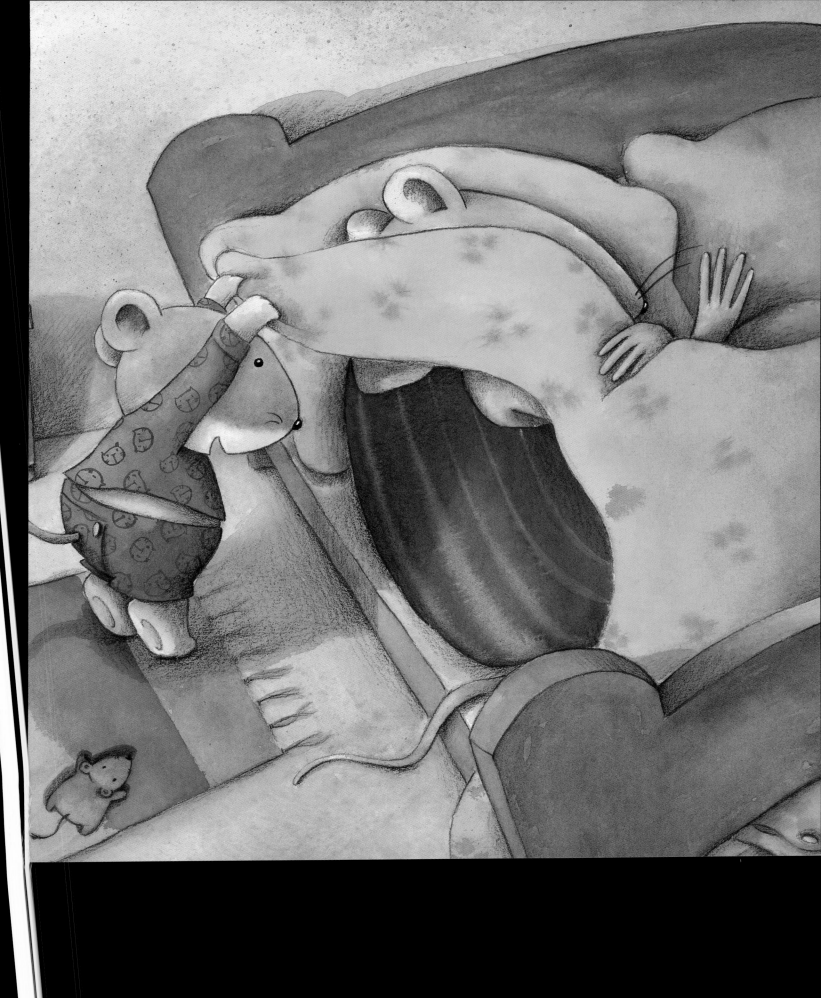

Miko took Mom's alarm clock with him. When the small hand came around to the same spot as the red alarm hand, it would ring. But he had to think of something to do until then.

Miko tumbled around on the floor.

Then he sat completely still.

Miko even tried to figure out which finger was the best for picking his nose.

But when he looked at the clock,
the small hand had barely moved.
Miko sighed, "Now what?"

"I know. I'll look at my books!" said Miko.
"It's too bad that Mom wants to sleep, because she loves stories as much as I do."
Miko put Mom's favorite books off to the side.
"When she wakes up, we can read them together!"

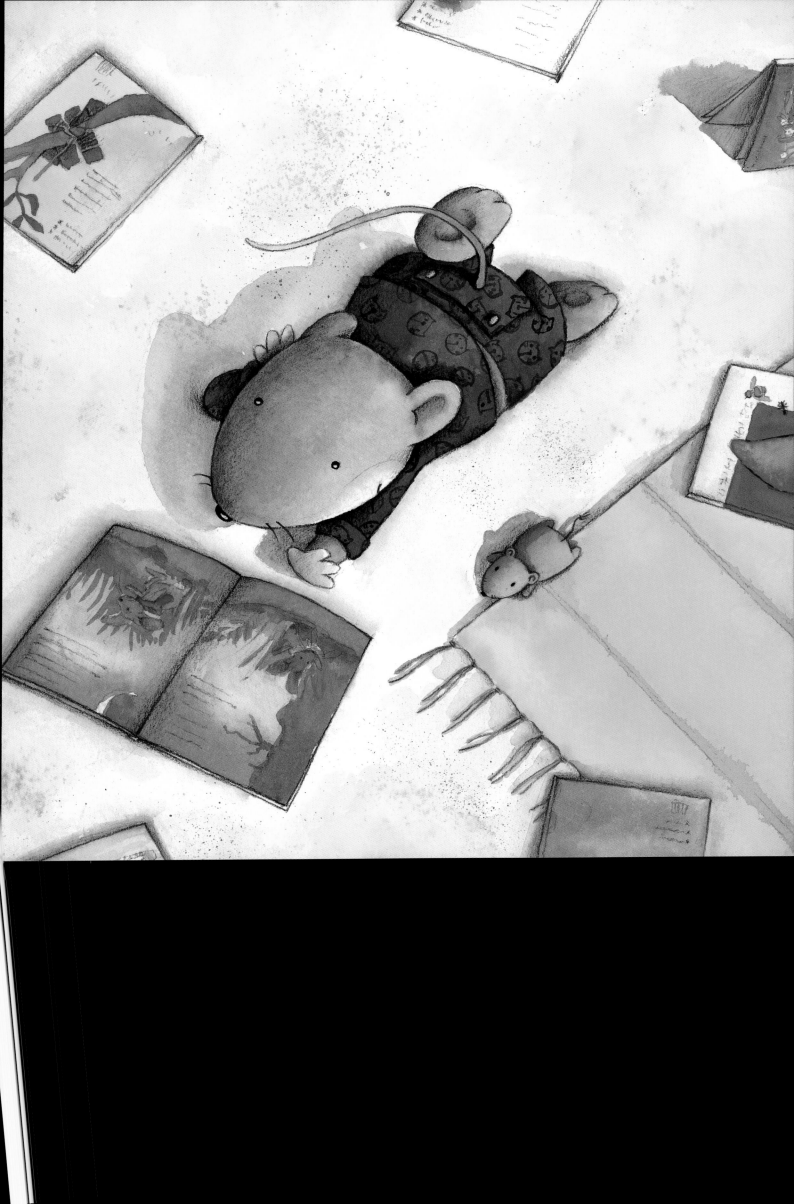

Suddenly, Miko heard a noise. "GNURR!"
"What is that?" Miko looked under his bed,
but no one was there, except an old smelly sock.

Then he heard the sound again. "GNURR!"
Miko laughed. "My stomach is growling! How funny!
Let's go and tell Mom. Oh, no, we can't until the alarm rings...
Mimiki, let's get something to eat."

Miko found a big juicy apple.

"Delicious!" he said, smacking his lips.

"It's too bad that Mom wants to sleep, because she loves apples as much as I do."

Miko only ate half of his apple.

"When Mom wakes up, we can eat the other half together!"

Miko pulled out his toys so he could play.
"It's too bad that Mom wants to sleep,
   because she loves to play with my toys as much as I do."
   Miko set up his figures all across his bed.
"When Mom wakes up, we can play with them together!"
   Miko looked at the clock, but the hands were not together yet.
"Oh my," sighed Miko. "Now what can I do?"

"I know. I'll make a surprise for Mom!"

Miko cut colored paper and pasted ribbons.
"I have to hurry," he said. "It's almost time!"

Quietly, Miko tiptoed into Mom's room.
He put the surprise next to her. Then, he waited.

It will happen soon...

"Rrrrrʀʀʀ-ing! Rrrrrrrʀ-ing! Rrrrrrʀʀ-ing!"

Mom jumped up!
"I wrapped up some time for you to sleep,"
   smiled Miko. "Was it a good idea?"
"Of course!" Mom said with a giggle.
"Now I'm rested and ready to play!"
   She gave Miko a big good morning kiss.

"Come on, Mom," said Miko
   taking her by the hand.

"I want to show you all the things I thought of that we can do together. Now that you're awake, we have lots of time to play!"

For more information about MIKO and our other books and the authors and artists who created them, please visit our website: **www.minedition.com**